Dear Parent:
Your child's love of reading starts here!

I Can Read Books have introduced children to the joy of reading since 1957. Featuring award-winning authors and illustrators and a fabulous cast of beloved characters, I Can Read Books set the standard for beginning readers. From books your child reads with you to the first books they read alone, there are I Can Read Books for every stage of reading:

SHARED READING
Basic language, word repetition, and whimsical illustrations, ideal for sharing with your emergent reader

BEGINNING READING
Short sentences, familiar words, and simple concepts for children eager to read on their own

READING WITH HELP
Engaging stories, longer sentences, and language play for developing readers

READING ALONE
Complex plots, challenging vocabulary, and high-interest topics for the independent reader

ADVANCED READING
Short paragraphs, chapters, and exciting themes for the perfect bridge to chapter books

Every child learns in a different way and at their own speed. Some read through each level in order. Others go back and forth between levels and read favorite books again and again. You can help your young reader improve and become more confident by encouraging their own interests and abilities.

A lifetime of discovery begins with the magical words, **"I Can Read!"**

HarperCollins®, ☕®, and I Can Read Book®
are trademarks of HarperCollins Publishers Inc.

The Berenstain Bears' Seashore Treasure
Copyright © 2005 by Berenstain Bears, Inc.
For information address HarperCollins Children's Books,
a division of HarperCollins Publishers,
195 Broadway, New York, NY 10007.
www.harperchildrens.com
Library of Congress Cataloging-in-Publication Data
Berenstain, Stan.
    The Berenstain Bears' seashore treasure / Stan & Jan Berenstain.—1st ed.
      p.   cm.— (An I can read book)
    Summary: When the Bear family goes to the seashore, they find a map which they hope will lead
them to buried treasure.
    ISBN 978-0-06-058341-5 (pbk.)—ISBN 978-0-06-058340-8 (lib bdg.)
    [1. Seashore—Fiction. 2. Buried treasure—Fiction. 3. Bears—Fiction.] I. Berenstain, Jan. II. Title.
III. Series.
PZ7.B4483Bffm 2005
[E]—dc22   200414424
                                                                                           CIP
                                                                                            AC

Typography by Scott Richards

16 SCP 10 9 8 7

First Edition

I Can Read!

BEGINNING READING 1

The Berenstain Bears'
SEASHORE
TREASURE

WITHDRAWN

Stan & Jan Berenstain

HarperCollinsPublishers

The Bear family was going to the seashore.

They were going across a bridge.

The bridge went to Laughing Gull Island.

It was called Laughing Gull Island

because so many laughing gulls lived there.

"*Ha! Ha! Ha!*" cried the laughing gulls

as they sailed across the sky.

"Will we be there soon?" asked Sister Bear.

"Yes," said Papa Bear.

"Do you see that house on the beach?

That is where we are going to stay."

The Bear family unpacked the car.

They carried their things into the house.

Brother, Sister, and Papa Bear

put on their swimsuits.

Mama decided to wait until later.

"Come, Papa," said Brother.

"Let's go to the beach."

"Hmm," said Papa.

"I found something in the closet."

"What is it?" asked Brother.

"It is a map," said Papa.

"An old pirate treasure map."

"Really, my dear," said Mama.

"It says this place used to be called

Pirates Cove!" said Papa.

"It says that pirates buried their booty here."

"What is booty, Papa?" asked Sister.

"It is treasure," said Papa.

"Pirate treasure. You know—gold, silver, diamonds, and rubies."

"Now, really, my dear," said Mama.

"Do you think the map is real?"

asked Brother.

"There's only one way to find out,"

said Papa. "Follow me."

Papa got a shovel.

They went down to the beach.

It was a bright sunny day.

The sea sparkled.

Waves crashed upon the shore.

"Ha! Ha! Ha!" cried the laughing gulls.

Papa began to dig.

The cubs splashed in the sea.

"Have you found any treasure yet, Papa?"

asked Brother.

"Not so far," said Papa.

"All I have found are some old shells."

"What is this one, Papa?"

asked Sister.

"That is a clam shell," said Papa.

"It is big and gray," said Sister.

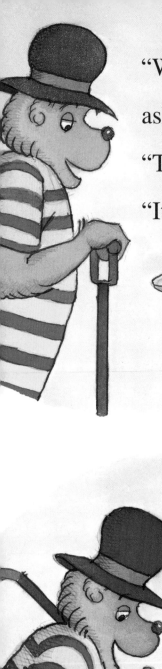

"What is this one?"

asked Brother.

"That is an oyster shell,"

said Papa.

"It is bumpy and black,"

said Brother.

Papa looked at the treasure map.

"Hmm," he said.

"This must not be the right spot."

He moved to another spot

and dug some more.

"Any treasure yet, Papa?"

asked Brother.

"No, just more old shells," said Papa.

"What is this one?"

asked Brother.

"That is a scallop shell,"

said Papa.

"It is pretty and pink,"

said Sister.

"What are shells for?" asked Brother.

"Shells are the homes

of some sea animals," said Papa.

"The clam shell was the home of a clam.

The oyster shell was the home of an oyster.

The scallop shell was the home of a scallop."

The sun shone down.

The sea sparkled.

Waves crashed upon the shore.

"Ha! Ha! Ha!" cried the laughing gulls.

"Papa, what happened to the clam, the oyster, and the scallop?" asked Sister.

"I guess maybe the laughing gulls got them," said Papa.

Papa looked at the map again.

"Hmm," he said.

"This must not be the right spot."

He went to another spot

and dug some more.

"Any treasure yet, Papa?" asked Sister.

"I'm afraid not," said Papa.

"Just some more old shells."

"You know something?" said Papa.

"Digging for treasure is hot work!"

"*Ha! Ha! Ha!*" cried the laughing gulls.

"Hmm," said Papa.

"Do you think those gulls are laughing at us and our treasure hunt?"

"No way!" said Brother.

"We came looking for treasure
and we found it.

We found *the treasure of the sea*!"

"That's right," said Sister.

"A whole bucket full!"

"Time for a dip!"

said Papa.

After they cooled off
they headed back to the house
to show Mama their treasure.

"Papa," said Brother, "what are you going to do with the treasure map?"

"Hmm," said Papa, "I may just leave it in the closet for the next papa bear."